The Flintstones® are a registered trademark of
Hanna-Barbera Productions, Inc.
Copyright © 1994 by Turner Publishing, Inc.
All rights reserved.
First Edition 10 9 8 7 6 5 4 3 2
ISBN: 1-57036-144-4
Illustrated by VACCARO ASSOCIATES, INC.
Printed and bound in the U.S.A.

The Flintstones Stone Age Fairy Tales

The Reluctant Dragon

··

Jack and the Beanstalk

INTRODUCTION

What would you say to a Fairy or Sprite?
Who dances up moonbeams on a cold winter night?
Would you believe that Dragons take flight?
To search for brave Knights with whom they can fight?

Do you know of a Giant who's as big as a house?
Or a Wizard who turns quickly into a mouse?
Are there Witches on broomsticks flying tonight?
Are Trolls under bridges—well out of sight?

Can a bullfrog ever be really a Prince?
Do Leprechauns vanish when put in a pinch?
Are Unicorns always shy, gentle, and wise?
Does a Fox ever dress in human disguise?

If you would know answers to questions like these,
Then just turn the page as fast as you please.
For as sure as wishes and dreams come true,
A fairyland adventure is waiting for you.

THE RELUCTANT DRAGON

Once upon a time, there was a small village tucked away among the rolling green hills of old England. And like most little villages it was, for the most part, a peaceful and quiet place. Not very much of anything ever happened to cause even a stir of outrage, delight, or just plain curiosity.

That is, until the *dragon* came.

The dragon had taken up residence in a cave on top of a hill overlooking the village. No one knew where the dragon had come from, or how he came to be so near their village. The fact that he was a dragon, and knowing full well what dragons like to do best, sent a shudder of fear through every villager. They imagined the dragon swooping down from his perch on the hill, burning their crops and destroying their homes.

Something would have to be done, and done quickly, before the beast could do his worst.

But indeed,
nothing could have been
further from this dragon's
thoughts. He didn't care a bit for
rampaging, pillaging, or plundering.
Why the very idea of breathing fire upset him,
for it would most certainly lead to a sore throat.
No, this dragon was *different*.
The prospect of bringing pain and misery to anyone was simply
beyond this dragon's understanding. He'd much rather smell the sweet
spring flowers, enjoy a soothing sunset, or, best of all, write poetry. This
dragon adored poetry and spent most of his time reading and writing it!
And to tell the truth, his poems weren't half bad.

But to the villagers down below, he was always the *terrible* dragon. That, since his arrival, he had done nothing wicked or wily, whatsoever, didn't make a bit of difference to them. It was only a matter of time, the townsfolk said, before this beast would begin to behave badly.

So, the elders of the village gathered together to decide what to do about this terrifying beast. They talked, and talked, and talked, until it became quite clear that no one was brave enough to challenge this dragon. Finally, it was decided they would seek the services of the brave knight, Sir George, the Dragonslayer. This dragon, enjoying the delightful day and reading a bit of verse, spied Sir George in the distance. He thought the knight made a gallant sight on his galloping steed and was considering writing a verse or two about the fellow, when suddenly Sir George crested the hill.

"Ho there, Dragon!" called Sir George.

"Well, ho there to you," replied the dragon.

Sir George cleared his throat, "Dragon! I have come on behalf of..."

"Now listen here," interrupted the dragon, "don't hit me, throw stones, squirt water, or do anything of the kind. I won't have it, I tell you! I won't!"

"Hold it, hold it! You are a dragon, are you not?" Sir George cried.

"I most certainly am," replied the dragon.

"Well, then you know why I'm here. So don't give me any trouble." said Sir George.

"If you mean to fight me, fellow, well, you can just forget it," said the dragon. "True, I am a dragon, but I am also a gentleman and I don't care a bit for roughhousing. So, good day, sir!"

Sir George was very surprised, and confused. "He had never met a dragon quite like this one.

"But what if I make you fight?" demanded the knight.

"You can't," said the dragon, smiling. "If you try I will simply go into my cave and stay there! You'll soon get quite tired of waiting for me to come out and fight you. And when you do go away, I'll come out again. For, you see, I like it here, and here I will stay."

Sir George thought for a moment.

"I can see you're a respectable fellow," said Sir George. "If it were up to me, I would leave you alone, and that would be that. But the villagers expect a fight. If you don't fight me, they'll just send someone else to take my place. Unless..."

"Yes? Unless, what?" asked the dragon, who, by this time, was quite upset

with the whole unpleasant business.
"Unless you and I were to have a make-believe battle!
You could huff and puff smoke, breathe fire,
and generally stamp about while I pretend to
attack and defeat you in this little battle of ours.
It just might work!"
"If I do this," said the dragon, "you'd be sure
to mind where you poke that spear?"
Sir George promised to be careful, and the
two shook hands, agreeing to meet in the
morning to carry out their plan.

The next day, the entire village arrived for the battle. Sir George appeared upon his mighty steed, lance in hand. But attention was soon drawn to the cave. A thunderous roar bellowed from the opening. The ground began to shake and quake and, in the next moment, the dragon emerged. He stamped about in a frightful rage, as fireballs shot from his mouth and thick smoke blew from his flaring nostrils. He was a terrible sight to behold.

"Boy," thought Sir George, "I hope the dragon remembers our plan."

The two mighty warriors fought throughout the misty morning. However, neither the dragon nor Sir George were really hurt. The dragon did receive a stinging rap to his nose when Sir George came too close with a punch. And Sir George's bottom received a bit of a scorching when the dragon blew a fireball with a little too much might. But for the most part, neither was the worse for wear.

Finally, the dragon pretended to beg for mercy as he fell in defeat from one of Sir George's blows. Sir George then gave the dragon a good talking-to. The dragon promised never to burn, pillage, plunder, or rampage their village.

No, not ever!

Quite satisfied with the whole affair, the villagers called for a feast in honor of the victorious Sir George—and the defeated dragon.

The banquet was a grand affair that continued long into the starlit night. The dragon told jokes, recited poetry, and impressed the villagers with his well-traveled tales and far-flung adventures. Sir George was very happy to have met *this* dragon. The dragon was never happier, as he now had many new friends. For you see, the dragon, above all, was quite lonely.

But the night was growing old, and it was well past everyone's bedtime. "Sir George," said the dragon, "would you mind terribly if I asked you to walk me home?"

"Not at all, dragon. Have you forgotten your way?"

"No, no. Not quite," whispered the dragon. "Now, I wouldn't want this to get around, but I'm frightfully afraid of the dark. You understand, my friend, don't you?"

"Yes, yes, come on!" said Sir George, laughing, and the two new friends climbed the hill toward the dragon's home. And throughout the whole valley on that wondrous night, everyone could hear the dragon and Sir George singing a jolly song.

JACK AND THE BEANSTALK

There once was a poor widow who had a son named Jack. They lived in a small cottage not far from a little village. The winter had been very hard for them and, by spring, there was not a scrap of food left to eat.

"Come here, son," the mother called. Jack was a good and thoughtful boy, so he went at once to his mother's side. "We have nothing left to eat," the widow said with a sigh, "and we have no money to buy food. You will have to take Daisy to the village market and sell her—or we shall starve."

Daisy was their cow, and the family's last possession.

Jack reluctantly did as he was told. Placing a rope around Daisy's neck, he set off down the road with her toward the village market.

Along the way Jack met a very strange-looking man.
"My, my, my just look at this fine cow you have" said the man. "I'll bet
you're off to the market to sell her, eh? Good lad, but might I make you
an offer, first?"
The man pulled from his pocket five little beans.
"Look close, my boy," the man began, "I will trade for this fine cow of
yours these five magic beans." Then he sang:

"All of your wishes and most of your dreams,
Shall be granted to you by five little beans.
Life's many troubles strike weak and strong,
And trouble cares not for right or wrong.

"But if you are good, and if you are brave,
These five little beans will pave your way.
Take them, my boy, take them in hand,
Trust in the magic at your command!"

Jack happily swapped Daisy for the beans and hurried home to his mother. "Back so soon, Jack?" asked his mother in amazement. "Well, I hope you got a good price for poor Daisy. Come show me. How much money did she bring at the market?"

Jack proudly opened his hand to show his mother the five magic beans. "What?! Beans?" cried Jack's mother. "You traded Daisy for a handful of beans? How could you, Jack? Oh, my boy, what have you done? We shall surely starve now!" and she went inside the cottage to cry.

Jack had never felt more foolish. Magic beans indeed! He was tempted to throw the horrid beans as far as he possibly could. But Jack thought better of it. At least the beans might give them something to eat this spring. He dug a little hole in the garden and dropped the beans in. Then he carefully covered them with dirt and watered them. Ashamed, Jack went to his room and sobbed himself asleep.

The next morning, Jack rose early and went to greet the day at his window. Looking out, he could hardly believe his eyes. Where he had planted the five little beans there was now an enormous beanstalk! Enormous, why, it curled high above the cottage, up above the tallest mountain, and up through the clouds!

Jack wasted no time, and before his mother awoke, he quickly ran outside and began climbing the beanstalk. He knew now that the beans were magic, and that he must find out what was at the top of the beanstalk. He climbed, and climbed, and climbed! Before long, Jack was high above the valley and among the clouds. Still the beanstalk went higher!

When, at last, Jack reached the top of the beanstalk,
he found himself in a strange and wonderful land.
Glistening golden fields stretched out before him,
ending at the edge of a dark and towering forest.
Jack could see a colossal castle off in the
distance and wondered what kind of people
lived in this land high above the clouds.
Jack made his way to the castle and
standing before its door, he realized that
this castle was not just big, it was the
biggest! The castle door was huge! It
stood some thirty feet high. Jack gave
a little shudder thinking of who lived
in such a place. He took courage,
though, remembering what the
strange man had told him:
"If you are good, and if you are brave,
These five little beans will pave your way."

He squeezed himself under the door. Jack knew now that this land above the clouds was a land of giants.

Once inside, Jack made his way down a long hall and into an enormous dining room. In the dining room was a huge table, and on this table was food. Lots of food. The biggest-sized food Jack had seen in all his life! He decided at once to climb a leg of the table and gather as much food as possible to bring back to his poor mother. Jack had reached the top of the table when he felt it begin to shake and he heard what sounded like thunder. The sound grew louder and louder. Boom...Boom...Boom...BOOM!

Then he heard a deep voice say:

"Fee-fie-fo-fum!
I smell the blood of an Englishman.
Be he alive, or be he dead,
I'll grind his bones to make my bread."

Upon hearing this, Jack jumped into the sugar bowl to hide. Just in time, for at that moment a giant appeared. The giant had been busy all morning stealing cattle, tearing up crops, trampling on people's homes, and generally doing what giants like to do best. Needing a break from his work, he'd decided to come home to eat a giant meal and take a giant nap. But as soon as he entered the castle, his nostrils filled with a peculiar smell.

The giant looked everywhere, but he couldn't find Jack. Before long, the aroma of dinner overwhelmed the giant's attention, and he sat down to eat. When he was through with his meal, the giant took down his two most prized possessions: a hen that laid golden eggs and a beautiful harp that sang with the voice of an angel. The giant commanded the hen to lay three golden eggs. One, two, three golden eggs appeared. Pleased with the hen, the giant then commanded the harp to sing as he settled down for a nap. He soon fell fast asleep to the gentle voice of the harp. With the giant asleep, Jack snuck out of the sugar bowl and tiptoed across the table.

Suddenly it occurred to him that he would not need to steal food if he had a hen that laid golden eggs. Reaching the hen, Jack grabbed her and began to make his way to the edge of the table. Just before he started down, the harp sang out to him:
"Brave boy, brave boy, don't leave without me,
A prisoner I am of the giant you see.
Take me away from this ogre with you,
And I'll sing pretty tunes all your days through."

Jack was about to return for the harp when the giant began to stir. He quickly hid behind the bowl of fruit. The giant said sleepily:

"Fee-fie-fo-fum!
I smell the blood. . .ahhh!. . .of an Englishman."

The giant rubbed his eyes a bit and cleared his throat.

"Be he alive, or be he dead,
I'll grind his bones to make my bread.
Hee, hee, oh yes, yes, I will, I surely will."

The giant fell
back asleep.

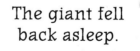

Jack acted quickly, and running back across
the table, he scooped the harp up under one arm, as
he held the hen tightly under the other. He had almost
made it to the edge of the table when he slipped on a pat of
butter. The harp cried out as they fell, and the giant awoke.
Without losing his grip on either hen or harp, Jack jumped
from the table and ran for the door.
"I knew it! I knew it!" the giant cried in anger. "You won't
escape me, little man." And the giant began to chase after Jack.
Jack made it safely to the beanstalk, but only because the giant
tripped twice over his own huge feet. With the hen on his head
and the harp under one arm, Jack began to climb down the
beanstalk. The giant peered down through the clouds and,
seeing Jack, began to climb down after him.

Jack reached the bottom ahead
of the giant, but with huge strides
the giant was only moments away from
overtaking him. Jack quickly set the hen
and harp down and grabbed an ax. When
his mother ran from the cottage to greet
him, she let out a cry as she saw the giant
lumbering down upon them.
Jack chopped away at the beanstalk with all
his might, until he cut it clean in two. The stalk
gave way and came crashing down.
Oh, noooooo!" screamed the giant as he
covered his eyes, facing a nasty fall to earth.
But luckily, for the giant, the beanstalk fell out
over the nearby sea. No one knew if he could
swim, but, at any rate, the
giant was never
seen again.

Jack, his mother, the hen, and the harp lived
a very long and happy life together.